KU-201-652

# THIS BOOK BELONGS TO

~~Dennis~~          ~~Sharralanda~~

...........................................................

...........................................................

**LADYBIRD BOOKS**

UK | USA | Canada | Ireland | Australia | India | New Zealand | South Africa

Ladybird Books is part of the Penguin Random House group of companies
whose addresses can be found at global.penguinrandomhouse.com.

www.penguin.co.uk   www.puffin.co.uk   www.ladybird.co.uk

 Penguin
Random House
UK

First published 2021
005

Text and illustrations copyright © Ludo Studio Pty Ltd 2021

BLUEY (word mark and character logos) are trade marks of Ludo Studio Pty Limited and are used under licence.
BLUEY logo © Ludo Studio Pty Limited 2018. Licensed by BBC Studios. BBC is a trade mark of the
British Broadcasting Corporation and is used under licence. BBC logo BBC © 1996

Adapted by Rebecca Gerlings

Printed in the United Kingdom

The authorized representative in the EEA is Penguin Random House Ireland,
Morrison Chambers, 32 Nassau Street, Dublin D02 YH68

A CIP catalogue record for this book is available from the British Library

ISBN: 978-0-241-48694-8

All correspondence to:
Ladybird Books, Penguin Random House Children's
One Embassy Gardens, 8 Viaduct Gardens, London SW11 7BW

**MIX**
Paper from
responsible sources
**FSC** www.fsc.org   FSC® C018179

# BLUEY

# THE BEACH

Bluey, Bingo, Mum and Dad are off to the beach.

They set up the tent, roll around in the sand and then race to the water.

Bluey and Bingo pretend that the waves are trying to splash them.

Here comes a BIG one!

Mum sets off for a walk along the beach.
"Why do you like walking by yourself?" asks Bluey.

"I'm not sure," says Mum. "I just do.
See you soon, little mermaid."
*What a strange answer*, thinks Bluey.

Just then, Bluey finds a beautiful
shell in the sand.
"Can I go and show Mum?" she asks.
"All right, off you go," says Dad.

"For real life?" says Bluey. "All by myself?"
Dad nods. "Yeah, just don't go in the water."

Bingo waves her hands over Bluey's tail.
Bluey laughs. "I am the mermaid who got her legs!"

Mum is now a tiny orange speck.
Bluey frowns. "Maybe I'll just stay here with you and Dad."
"But, little mermaid, you can follow Mum's footsteps," says Bingo.
"Oh yeah!" Bluey grins. "Thanks!"

Bluey SKIPS across the sand towards Mum.
"I am the mermaid who got her legs!"
She laughs. "But only for a day!"

She CARTWHEELS and *RUNS* along the shore
until she almost BUMPS into some . . .

. . . Seagulls! "Um, can you please move?" Bluey
asks politely. "A mermaid needs to get through."

But the seagulls don't budge.

It's a good thing mermaids aren't scared of seagulls!

Bluey laughs as she H<sup>O</sup>PS from one footprint to another until . . .

# CRASH!

A **BIG** wave sneaks up and crashes on to the shore. It takes Mum's footsteps out to sea.

"Ooh, you cheeky wave!" Bluey barks.
"How will I find Mum now?"

Just as Bluey begins to lose hope, she
spots a pipi coming up for wee-wees!

HEE!
HEE!
HEE!

Then a crab scuttles past.
Bluey copies its funny sideways walk.
"I am the mermaid who got her crab legs!"

PINCHY!
PINCHY!

ARGHH!

Bluey scampers away. But then she sees a . . .

"Jellyfish! How will I get past?" Bluey says,
picking up a stick. She pokes the blue blob.

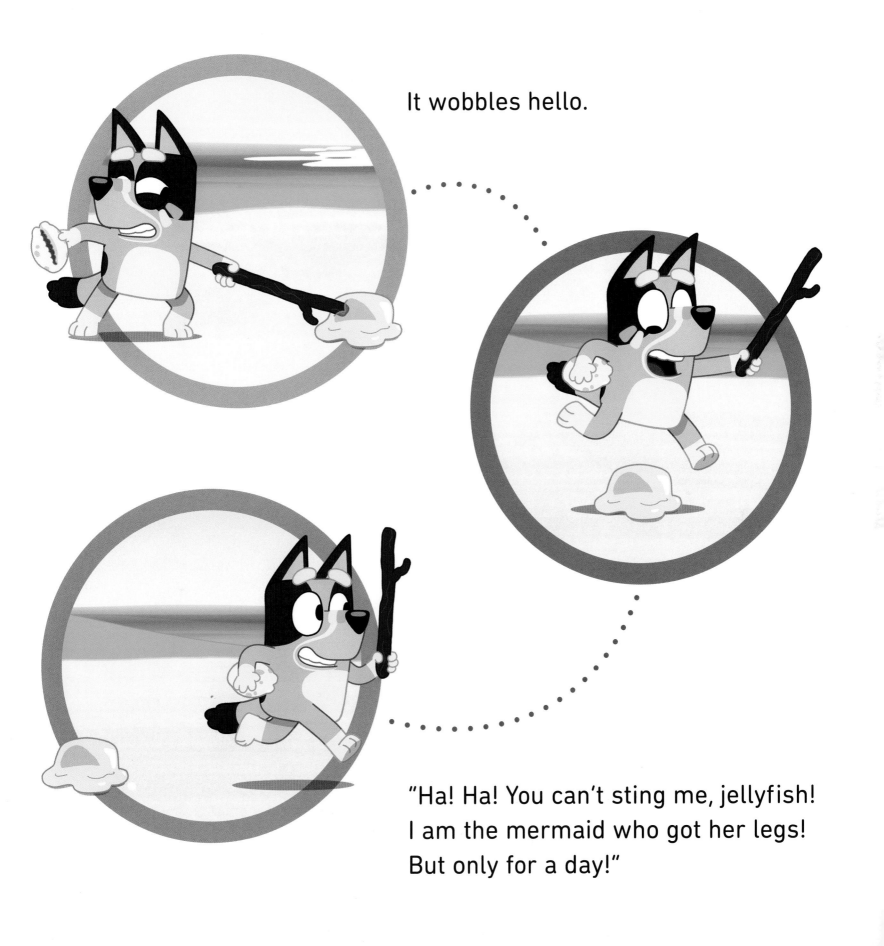

It wobbles hello.

"Ha! Ha! You can't sting me, jellyfish!
I am the mermaid who got her legs!
But only for a day!"

Bluey races ahead.
"Look at this amazing shell!" she calls, but Mum's still too far away to hear. Better keep going!

MUM!

Bluey stops at an old sandcastle.
"I wonder who lives here?" she gasps, peeping through the windows. "Maybe this is where the other mermaids live."

She leaves her stick as a present and
backs away until she bumps right into a . . .

. . . Pelican!

"Um, would you mind moving?"
Bluey asks. "I need to show
this shell to my mum."

ARGHH!

But the pelican doesn't budge.

Bluey thinks she's had enough of walking by herself now.
She glances back at Dad, but he's just a tiny blue speck.

"If I can't go backwards, and I can't go forwards, **what am I going to do?**"

Bluey remembers the seagulls and crabs and the jellyfish. If she managed to get past them, maybe she can get past a pelican, too . . .

She summons every bit of courage. After all, a little mermaid has got to be brave.

"I am THe MeRMaID WHO GOT HeR LeGS! BUT ONLY FOR a Day!"

Then she tiptoes around the pelican.

SQUAWK!

The pelican beats his great
big wings and flies away.

THANK YOU FOR
MOVING, MR PELICAN!

A familiar voice floats towards Bluey.
She gasps and spins around.

MUM!

BLUEY!

"Did you come all this way by yourself?"
asks Mum. "You little star!"

Bluey holds the shell to Mum's ear.
It has the whole beach inside it.

Bluey and Mum head back together.
"I **love** walking by myself," says Bluey.
"Oh yeah – why's that?" asks Mum.
It's a hard question. There are almost
too many reasons to say.
"I don't know. I just do."